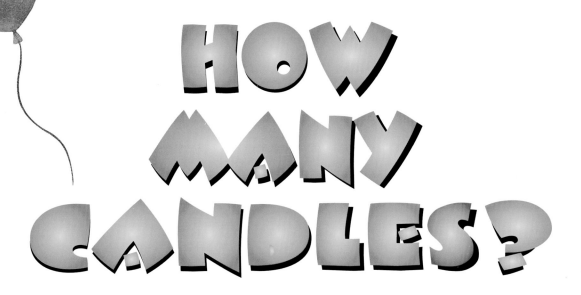

HOW MANY CANDLES?

BY HELEN V. GRIFFITH
PICTURES BY SONJA LAMUT

GREENWILLOW BOOKS NEW YORK

Egg tempera and oil paints were used for the full-color art.
The text type is Egyptian 505.
Text copyright © 1999 by Helen V. Griffith
Illustrations copyright © 1999 by Sonja Lamut
www.williammorrow.com
Printed in Hong Kong by South China Printing Company (1988) Ltd.
First Edition   10 9 8 7 6 5 4 3 2 1

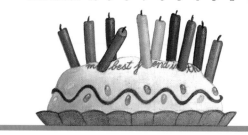

Library of Congress Cataloging-in-Publication Data
Griffith, Helen V.
How many candles? / by Helen V. Griffith ; pictures by Sonja Lamut.
p.   cm.
Summary: On the occasion of Robbie's tenth birthday,
a dog, cat, turtle, and bunch of gnats discuss how
that age compares with their own expected longevity.
ISBN 0-688-16258-4 (trade).   ISBN 0-688-16259-2 (lib. bdg.)
[1. Longevity—Fiction.   2. Animals—Fiction.
3. Birthdays—Fiction.]   I. Lamut, Sonja, ill.
II. Title.   PZ7.G8823Ho   1999
[E]—dc21   98-38958   CIP   AC

A book for Anne Wang
—H. V. G.

For my daughter, Anna
—S. L.

"What's the cake for?" asked the cat.
"Robbie's tenth birthday," said Alex.

"Ten years is a long time," said the cat. "Ten years in a boy is the same as seventy years in a cat."

"Does that mean I need
seventy candles?"
asked Alex.

"Seventy candles for what?"
asked a turtle.
He saw the cat and slapped
himself into his shell.

"I'm celebrating Robbie's
tenth birthday," said Alex.

"Ten years is nothing,"
said the turtle from
inside his shell.

"A ten-year-old boy is like a
seventy-year-old cat," said Alex.

"Seventy years is nothing," said the turtle.

"Turtles live to be one hundred," explained the cat.

"Are you one hundred?" Alex asked the turtle.

"I'm ten," said the turtle.

"Just like Robbie," said Alex.

iend in the whole world

"Not quite,"
   said the cat.
"Ten years to a turtle
   is eight years to a boy."
   Alex looked at the turtle.
   He looked at the cake.
   He looked at the cat.
"Does that mean two less
   candles?" he asked.

Two gnats were flying in circles
around Alex's head.
"What's the cake for?" they asked.
"Robbie is ten years old today,"
Alex told them.
"Nothing lasts that long,"
said the gnats.

"Turtles live to be one hundred," said Alex.
  The gnats looked at each other.
"Let's not listen," they said.
  They flew away, frowning at Alex
  over their shoulders.
"I don't think they believed me," said Alex.
"Well, they're gnats," said the cat.
"Ten years to a boy is
  one billion years
  to a gnat."

"Are you sure?" asked Alex.

"Not really," said the cat.

"That's good," said Alex,

"because a billion candles
   on this cake would make
   it hard to see where it says,
   'Happy Birthday to Robbie,
   my best friend in the
   whole world.'"

"Very likely,"
   said the cat.

He sniffed the cake.
"This seems to be made
of dog biscuits," he said.
"Is that wrong?" asked Alex.
"It's unusual," said the cat.
"Did you see which way
that turtle went?"

"He followed the gnats," said Alex.

The cat took off through the grass.
"When you find them," Alex called
after him, "bring them back for cake."